Boss Kids

Titi Ramirez

NEWMAN SPRINGS PUBLISHING
320 Broad Street
Red Bank, NJ 07701

First originally published by Newman Springs Publishing 2024

ISBN 979-8-88763-722-8 (Paperback)
ISBN 979-8-88763-723-5 (Digital)

Printed in the United States of America

To all kids who aspire to be their own boss

Hi, I'm Jake, and this is my sister, Jill.

Today you'll learn how to become your own boss and prepare for your future. (Honestly, we just like to have our own money at the store to spend.)

Let us show you how we did it. It's best if you ask a grown-up for help. We asked our Titi, and she was excited to help us.

Before we asked Titi, we made a plan.

We collected sticks. Our Titi had thread and Saran wrap (the stuff she covers food with). Also, we got all the paint and old paper lying around the house. Oh, and a bucket with some water too.

First, we took the sticks and tied them together.
Then we covered them in the plastic wrap.

Guess it's good the teacher gives us so much homework.
Yeah, I guess you're right!
Next, we ripped up all the old graded papers and put them in the bucket with the water. Titi said it was awesome because we were recycling, but I was happy about getting rid of that D I got in math last week.

After, we squeezed out the paper really well to get the water out.

We then covered our creation with the squeezed-out paper and let it dry out.

We painted them after they dried. I mixed blue and white. Jill used pink and found glitter to put on top for hers.

Once the paint dried, we were able to ask Titi for her help.

Titi made us our own web store on the website bosskids. net and business cards. It's so cool giving them out to people.

Titi then took us around to places like doctors' and dentists' offices to give them our cards.

Titi even got us our own booth at a craft show where we
sold out!

We work hard every day to make new items to sell on our web store.

I even made a really cool tooth that a dentist bought for his office.

So if you have an idea and work hard, you can be a boss kid too!

Just like us!

Do you want a chance to be a boss?

Do you like to make arts or crafts? Do you make jewelry or clothes? Can you take pebbles and sticks and turn them into artwork? We have the place for you to have your own online store—having a parent sign you up will give you just that—plus a chance to be a main character in one of the boss kids' books. All while learning how to be a young entrepreneur.

WE ARE BOSS KIDS

About the Author

One day, Titi Ramirez was with her nephew. He said, "Titi, I want to be a boss like you and my dad." That's when she had an idea that would help him do just that—be his own boss. She made a decision that day to take this even further and make more boss kids the best way she knows how: through words of encouragement and belief in them. She believes the greatest ideas come from the minds of the youth, which she will continue to inspire and cherish the opportunities to do so.

To find her story and more, visit at BossKids.net.